D1541291

The

SMALLEST BOY
IN THE CLASS

by

JERROLD BEIM

illustrated by
Meg Wohlberg

WILLIAM MORROW AND CO.
NEW YORK 1949

Other Books by Jerrold Beim

TWELVE O'CLOCK WHISTLE

ANDY AND THE SCHOOL BUS

COUNTRY FIREMAN

Miss Smith was a teacher in school. "Good morning, Evelyn, good morning, Sandy," she said to the children when they came in the

morning. "How are you, Pris..."
But Miss Smith never finished
Priscilla's name because she heard
a great big noise from the hall.

"Bang! Bang! I'm going to shoot you!" someone shouted. In came a boy wearing a cowboy hat and holding two red guns. "Bang! Bang!" he yelled, but then he stopped because no one looked scared. "It's only Tiny!" the children said and they laughed. He made a lot of noise but he was the smallest boy in the class.

Tiny's real name was Jim. He hated being the smallest boy in the class. "When will I be big?" he asked his father and mother one night. "Some people are short,

some people are medium, and some people are tall," Tiny's father said. "You be patient. Some day you'll be big enough," his mother said.

Every morning when school began
the children told about something
that had happened the day before.
Priscilla told about her cat having
kittens. Sandy told about going

shopping with his mother. Jane told about a funny program she had seen on television. When it was his turn, Tiny got up and told something, too.

"I was walking home from school
and I met a big lion," Tiny said.
"The lion roared at me but I
pulled his tail and swung him
around my head. He got scared

and ran away." Everyone in the
class laughed and laughed. They
knew that Tiny was too little to
hold a lion by the tail and swing
him around his head.

Poor Tiny! He hated being little. When the children painted pictures, he always drew the biggest ones. An ocean liner! A giant! The tallest building in the world!

When the teacher asked a question, Tiny always raised his hand to give the answer first. He shouted so loud Miss Smith had to put her hands over her ears.

When the class went outside to play, Tiny always pushed his way first to the top of the slide. It made the other children mad. But it made Tiny feel big to be at the top first.

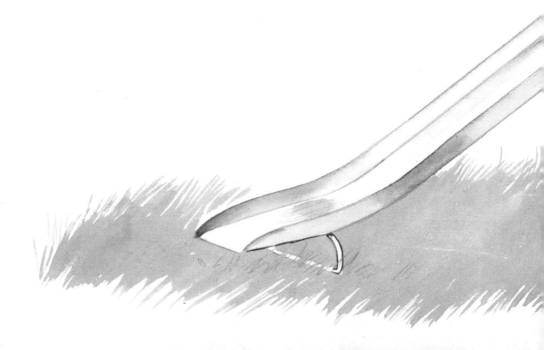

One day Miss Smith said, "We're all going on a trip tomorrow to visit a goat farm. Bring your lunches to school and we'll have a picnic on the farm." The children were so excited the next morning they could hardly do their lessons. Some of the mothers came in cars and drove everyone to the goat farm.

The goats were in a field and
there were big ones and little
ones. "Little goats are called

kids," the farmer told the children. Tiny put his hand out and patted a kid on the head. Priscilla started to pat one too, but then she noticed that her shoe-lace was untied.

"Wait a minute," Priscilla said to Tiny. She put her lunch down and started to tie her shoe.

"My lunch!" Priscilla cried. "The goat is eating it up!" They tried to take the lunch away from the goat, but it was too late. The goat ate it all—paper and string, too.

"It's time for our picnic now," Miss Smith called. "But I haven't anything to eat!" Priscilla cried. "The goat ate up my lunch." "Oh, that's too bad," Miss Smith said. "Won't you give Priscilla some of your lunch, Sandy?" she asked. "You have a big lunch." "No, I won't!" Sandy answered. "I need it all."

"Louise, you could give Priscilla one of your sandwiches, couldn't you?" Miss Smith said. Louise did not say anything but she held her box of lunch behind her back. Tears began to run down Priscilla's cheeks.

Tiny looked at her and it made him unhappy to see her cry. He thought about how hungry he was. Then he looked at Priscilla and saw the big tears on her cheeks. "Here," he said. "Here's a sandwich." Then he looked in his lunch box and pulled out a cookie. "Here's this," he said.

"Why, Jim, that's big of you!" Miss Smith exclaimed. "He isn't big. He's tiny!" Sandy said. "There's more than one way to be big," Miss Smith said. "It's big of him to give Priscilla part of his lunch. I think Jim must have the biggest heart of anyone in the class."

The biggest heart in the class!
The children all looked at Tiny
again. Miss Smith always knew
what was inside of things—in

clocks, in eggs, in frogs, in plants. And Miss Smith said that Tiny probably had the biggest heart of anyone in the class!

Everyone talked about the goat farm in school the next day, and they remembered what Miss Smith said about Tiny. Tiny remembered it, too.

Sometimes when he came to school in t

morning he still made the loudest noise.

He still drew the biggest pictures.

But sometimes he remembered there was another way to be big.

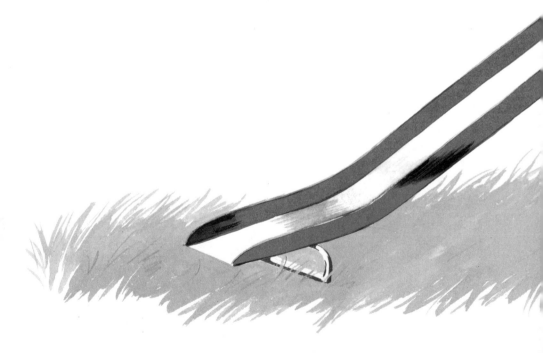

And one day the children forgot
to call him Tiny. "Come on, let's
play ball, Jim," they said.